Henry Beebee Carrington

Crisis Thoughts

Henry Beebee Carrington

Crisis Thoughts

ISBN/EAN: 9783337383367

Printed in Europe, USA, Canada, Australia, Japan

Cover: Foto ©Andreas Hilbeck / pixelio.de

More available books at **www.hansebooks.com**

CRISIS THOUGHTS.

BY

COL. HENRY B. CARRINGTON, U.S.A., M.A., LL.D.

"Disce, a priscis temporibus, solicitudinem pro futuro, habere."

PHILADELPHIA:

J. B. LIPPINCOTT & CO.

1878.

DEDICATION.

CONTENTS.

Contents

EXPLANATORY.

It is more than seventeen years since members of the Ohio Senate caused the first of these addresses to be repeated and published. It had been solemnly inspired by the conviction, publicly expressed, that " a war was impending which would outlast a presidential term, would cost hundreds of thousands of lives and thousands of millions of money." No blood had then been shed. The address was voluntary, and was illustrated by large maps of Pensacola and Charleston harbors, and diagrams of fortifications and ordnance. It was twice repeated, and before its last delivery Fort Sumter fell. Its republication has been requested by those whose judgment I respect. It was not at first the gush of a hasty impulse.

In 1836 a stranger visited a boarding-school at Torringford, Connecticut, which was conducted by Rev. Mr. Goodman and Dr. Radcliff Hudson, both of whom were afterwards mobbed in New England, for expressing anti-slavery opinions. The stranger explained to the class in geography, the nature and history of African slavery and the slave trade. He asked his listeners to stand up, if they were willing during after-years, to pray and labor for universal liberty. The stranger was John Brown, who departed this life at Charlestown, Virginia.

The impression made by that stranger was never effaced.

Certain violence at Farmington, Connecticut, in 1839, and at Columbus, Ohio, in 1849, incidentally referred to on page 83, only deepened that impression, and indicated that ultimate conflict, alone, would solve the maturing issue.

In February, 1861, Senator Chase thus addressed the writer, then adjutant-general of Ohio : "Our most sober thinkers, and those best informed, as well as conservative men from the South, predict war. Our militia should be officered by the wisest and best men. How soon they may be needed, no man can tell."

Mr. Cass, Secretary of State, in writing to the same officer, and referring to his own relations with President Buchanan, said, "We have indeed fallen upon evil times, when those who should preserve, seem bent upon destroying, the country."

The later addresses, to the soldiers of Indiana, on Washington's birthday, 1863, and to the colored people of Indianapolis, on the dedication of a church edifice, in 1869, are parts of one enforced. sequence..of convictions, which have proper place with the first address.

The *first* foreshadowed the struggle. The *second* contemplated a crisis in its progress. The *third* sought to win an emancipated race to right appreciation of so costly a deliverance.

As grouped, they testify of the dangers of political passion and the value of peace, at any honorable compromise of non-essentials, and appeal to parties, sections, and races " to learn from former experiences to have solicitude for the future," and thus unite, as did the Roman Senate in its supreme hour of peril, to " see that no harm shall befall the republic."

WABASH COLLEGE, CRAWFORDSVILLE, IND.,
July 4, A.D. 1878.

1*

THE HOUR: THE PERIL: THE DUTY.

DELIVERED AT COLUMBUS, OHIO, WHILE ADJUTANT-
GENERAL OF OHIO, APRIL 11 AND 17, 1861.

IN an hour like this, when the nervous wire thrills, each second, with some fresh note of alarm, when men hold their breath as they wait upon the electric flash, when minutes fulfil the work of hours, and each day is more fraught with issues vital to freedom and mankind than were months or years in earlier times, it is preeminently necessary that we meet each crisis squarely, weigh well our several obligations, and prove resolute for each and every duty or endeavor that may be forced against us.

Nor is any citizen or class of citizens exempt from a share of responsibility at such a time. None worthy the name will disclaim that responsibility, or fail to testify their interest. The man of daily labor pauses in his round of work to ask for the "last dispatch," and all trades and occupations, all crafts and callings, share in undefined but real apprehension as to our national future.

Could we rise above the trammels of party bias and personal concern, and, as lovers of

11

liberty and lovers of justice, calmly review the scenes which from hour to hour transpire wherever civilized man is now the actor, all that appears involved, or gloomy, would take order and unity, and would fill its fit place in the grand drama now being enacted, which will have as its catastrophe the end of despotism, and as its climax, the supremacy of liberty and right.

Could we rise to a still loftier height of observation, and perceive the hand of the Infinite, as with magic art and plastic touch it moulds the nations and bends the designs of men to the development of a Kingdom of Peace, we could even exult in all that now seems forbidding, or fatal to the public weal, and could behold, with all the assurance of prophecy itself, the dawning of a better day.

But the finite mind, as it gazes upon the swiftly-changing scenes, and traces the swelling volume of the plot, and the startling issues that boldly leap to view through each succeeding act, wearies with the complex mechanism and the confused purposes that mark the parts, until at length we dread each shift of scene, as if the Sixth Seal and the woes of the Apocalyptic vision were presently to be ushered upon the earth.

FREEDOM ADVANCES.

If we prove dull to the voice of history, and fail to see on all its records the signs of progressive growth, and the ultimate freedom of mankind; if we perceive not the accumulated power which Christianity herself has infused into each advancing Commonwealth or State: we have at least reached a period of human progress where, with all the confidence of the intrepid Galileo, we may exclaim, " The world moves," at last.

Not alone in science and art; not alone in æsthetic culture and social growth; not alone in material wealth and power; but in the freedom of the State, and freedom of the individual man himself, the world *moves*, onward, and upward.

REACTION BUT TEMPORARY.

Reaction, by a normal law of nature, may assert its tendency for a passing hour; and the rebound of an active principle may beget a transient pause in the onward sweep of Liberty to its culminating triumph. The task-master may, again and again, assert his divine right to appropriate and use the unrequited toil of his fellow-man. Legitimate revolution may seem barren of fruit, and the counterfeit may put on the mien of proud and defiant mastery. Liberty may take the guise of License, and Anarchy may usurp the name and garb of Liberty! But Time, which receives them all into her appropriating charge, will try them in a fiery crucible,—will evolve the pure and reject the false.

The world has been convulsed by dynastic

changes heretofore. The race has been confounded by strange and unnatural conflicts heretofore. Right, Liberty, and Religion have been the plaything or contempt of false friends and still falser foes, and the tyrant has appeared only to mature in strength in his struggle with the down-trodden and oppressed, and to ride triumphantly over the fairest hopes of the people, heretofore.

Rome and Greece, Gaul and Britain, Poland and Hungary, France and Germany, have passed through the furnace, seven times heated, and with unequal issue; but in all, and through all, the advance of the people toward Liberty and Peace, has been true to the promised destiny of the race. Even where old organisms retain their form and name, you will still behold a change of feature. That which was once asserted in the name of despotic sway, has put on the show of serving the people, only through some time-honored machinery of the State. From week to week, and from hour to hour, through trial and peril, and in all the changing phases of our social life, we read the fresh assurance, that the cause of Humanity and Right is drawing near its crowning triumph.

SIGNS OF PROGRESS.

Ten years ago, and no mortal foresight could have anticipated the momentous changes and brilliant trophies which now adorn and dignify the advancing cause. Then, it had been madness to prophesy that which has already become fruition. Then, hope deferred made the heart sick, and it seemed as if all continental progress was at an end. Now, look at the contrast.

The press whispers, and thrones tremble. At the dash of its pen, new policies are inaugurated, and new codes enacted. Senates and Chambers, Deputies and Congresses, and all other modern types of representation of the popular will, simply decline their sanction, or declare their enmity to acts of a despotic scope, and that which once was known only to the privy council, or some self-reliant tyrant, until its crushing weight fell upon the unresisting commons, now drops nerveless and harmless before the breath of debate.

Magna Charta was but the forerunner. Everywhere the Proclamation, the Ukase, the Hatti Sheriff, and the Edict, are letting down the throne to receive upon its platform of power the true sovereign, the PEOPLE.

ALL NATIONS PLAY THEIR PART.

China stands open to the world. Binding treaties pledge her to admit free speech, free press, and an untrammelled conscience, as part of her method and policy. Japan unbars her gates, and accepts all nations as her neighbors. India dissolves the restraints of caste, unites her boundaries by the railroad and the telegraph, and the long-lived oppression of a selfish corporation gives place to the benignant sway of the English constitution and laws. Even Africa, so long the scorn of nations, discloses vast fields for profitable culture, and welcomes commerce to her new traffic in the cotton and the cane.

Turkey renounces the sale of man, and the Christian becomes the equal of the child of Mahomet in the hall of litigation, the porch of the mosque, and the bazaar of trade.

Russia enfranchises her servile millions, and no longer dares refuse to the struggling Poles a liberal code, a representative Council, and the machinery of a healthy organization, to be officered and directed by men of their own race and language.

Austria, wellnigh bankrupt in name and credit, flies from canons, and consistories, and concordats, to find her only hope and life in the organized representation of the people themselves.

Hungary calmly but firmly accepts the offer as a matter of simple right; while Transylvania and Servia present the same demand with assurance of success. France grows strong, but only in the warmth of maturing freedom; and all continents are agitated, or upheaved, by the impending issue, in which Liberty shall surely triumph. True it is that the iron arm of despotism, wher-

ever and however energizing, still threatens the
well-being of every State and people, and this, no
matter how many disguises it assumes, that it
may protract the struggle and attain its will.

The Emperor of France is styled "Emperor,
by the will of the French." The new-born
Kingdom of Italy, fair of proportion, and regal
in beauty, seats upon her throne a sovereign
"King, by the will of the people." Thrones
become insignificant, and titles are but shadows!
The leaven of liberty is at work, forcing itself
even into the presence-chamber of the Vatican,
and compelling Hapsburg and Bourbon alike to
bend with respect to its sublime and persistent
progress.

But a few more conflicts with the barbarism
of wrong, a few more lances splintered with the
champions of the worn-out systems of feudal
times, and freedom shall become the law of
nations as it is the law of God. Fair pledges,
specious guarantees, temporizing shifts, may
defer the day; but it surely draws on apace.
Soon, in politics as well as in religion and ethics,
it will not satisfy the honest searcher after truth,
to style evil good, and good evil,—to pronounce
the bitter sweet, and the sweet bitter. But truth,
simple and unqualified, uncompromised away by
refinements of clique or party, undiluted by
selfish sacrifice of principle for temporary ends,
will live and flourish. You and I may or may

not survive the struggle that must usher in the final scene; but come it must, and come it will. Even on the American continent, this agitation has been recognized and felt. Mexico, and her sister republics of Spanish pedigree, have been turned upon the wheel of Fortune, until you can scarcely distinguish the sway of the patriot from the rule of the despot.

THE UNITED STATES NO LONGER A MERE SPECTATOR.

Heretofore, seemingly remote from these conflicts, our own beloved land has sympathized with all oppressed nations, while her benefactions have not been withheld, neither have any turned from her charity away. Kosciusko and Bozzaris, Bolivar and Kossuth, alike thanked God that America had a being. Ireland and Madeira were rescued in their hour of desolation and wasting, and with glad hearts and voices sent up their incense of prayer and praise to Him who hitherto had blessed us.

But this proud republic is no longer before the footlights, an eager but independent spectator. Just as the head turns dizzy, and the eye wearies with beholding nation after nation dragged through the bewildering maze of characters and conflicts, we, too, are hurled upon the stage, forced to become the centre of all eyes, and to be tested as to our loyalty to freedom, and our right to the exalted post of her standard-bearer.

Planted in the highway of nations, clasping the continent with our arms, bounding, as at one leap, to unparalleled culture, greatness, and power, yet proud and zealous for a still wider sweep of empire, even at the expense of principle and others' rights, we reach this dizzy pitch of greatness, only to seem poised for a fall, the more fatal if we prove recreant to our trust, as our pre-eminence has been the more distinguished.

ELEMENTS OF PRESENT TROUBLE.

Nor will I pause here to analyze critically the causes which have induced the peril; neither will I impose upon any class of men or measures the sole responsibility for the impending struggle. Few could relieve themselves from a share of the burden, while all should feel that they must gladly meet any sacrifice to regain the vantage ground already lost. And yet, before I treat of the issue which is most pressing, and express my humble judgment of the path of duty, which should be boldly traced, permit me to refer to certain grave considerations, which have made our present peril almost inevitable, while they have also supplied the elements and accessories of revolution and riot.

I. *Moral Principle Rejected by Politicians.*

The *first* disorganizing element that I shall notice lies in the prevalent assumption that our historic prestige and our present destination, as the experimental model of Republican institutions in the world, absolves us from allegiance to those laws and moral maxims, which we enjoin upon dependent States, and which are, indeed, the only solid basis of individual or natural greatness. This may be traced in our arrogant diplomacy with lesser States, our thirst for extended territory, our contempt for Indian treaties, and our subjection of all political issues, whether of a moral or economic nature, to the behests of mere action, policy, or party. History records no instance of true national greatness achieved at such sacrifice of substantial, genuine principle.

II. Tampering with the Union.

A *second* fatal assumption is, that the bond of Union has become so permanent, peaceful, and stable, that it can be tampered with at pleasure; that parties may even stake their existence or success upon Union or Disunion issues, for merely adventitious triumphs, and may at the same time take for granted that the Union will suffer no harm.

Threats of disunion have been made for many years; but more threats have been made for mere party effect than there are now disunionists in the land. If the entire people could realize that such a question can no more be trifled with,

without injury to the State, than private virtue
or private character can bear a like freedom
without degradation or taint, we should be more
careful to guard this jewel of our national honor,
at whatever sacrifice of party or place. Besides
this, the United States have not been compelled
to fight their way to present distinction at the
cost of constant sacrifice and pain. Our fathers
did indeed prove their valor and achieve their
freedom by the ordeal of fire ; and they, at least,
appreciated and honored the freedom thus attained. But for nearly half a century our country
has advanced, regardless alike of jealousy abroad
and any and all deliberate systems of development at home. It has grown of itself. With
government and institutions apparently permanent, with all the advantages of freedom in the
State, and a Christian civilization among the
people, and with unparalleled variety and rich-
ness of soil and mineral wealth, we have not
even developed our accumulating resources as
rapidly as Nature and Providence have brought
them to light.

We have come to consider our franchises, our
progress, and our destiny, as fixed quantities,
subject to such changes only as will perpetuate
and develop them. We disregard fundamental
axioms of national growth and unity, we despise
the idea of a higher law than passing expediency,
and rest upon the flattering conceit that nothing

can rend or shatter the political fabric here established.

Our strength, our wealth, our cultivation, and our liberty have made us arrogant, self-sufficient, and proud, and the fruit of this weakness we now gather in an abundant but baleful harvest of dissension, discord, and threatened dismemberment. We forget that Liberty, like chastity, is jealous of reproach, and can be conserved only by an unblemished and unsuspected carriage.

III. Thirst for Office.

Still another element that depreciates and defiles the body politic lies in the infatuation for office, which has become more wide-spread, importunate, and ruinous to public virtue than the world has before witnessed, and is nearly as fatal to the State as dissolution itself. It lies at the base of party affinities, shapes its policy, fights its battles, and demands its rewards. But woe to that party which, when it rises into place, is led to make mere party fealty the qualification for preferment to places of trust, rather than the intrinsic worth of the candidates themselves.

These evils—the banishment of moral principle from political action, the trifling with our liberties upon the conceit of their own inherent perpetuity, and thirst for political office—have grown with our growth, have driven thousands of our most patriotic citizens from the public service, and now threaten to utterly demoralize the people themselves, or to engender a morbid indifference to all issues but the party issues of the passing hour.

When the good and virtuous feel it a degradation to enter the political arena, it always augurs ill for the public weal, even although their isolation and neglect of duty cannot excuse them for their share of responsibility for the very consequences they deplore.

All these elements of mischief have had their share in the palsy which has seized the body politic and held it powerless at the feet of rebellion or factious opposition to law.

IV. Failure to Appreciate our Peril.

But there is yet *another* element *inherent* in a peaceful and law-abiding State, the operation of which facilitates *political* treason, while it insures the punishment of *other* crimes. Whatever may be the daring of *parties*, all alike profess allegiance to the fundamental law, and all good citizens are reluctant to believe in a systematic endeavor to overthrow it. This very regard for peace restrains them from stern preparatory measures for the suppression of organizations, which, after all, may show but the ebullition of hasty temper, indulged through the legitimate organs of free speech and a free press. The line is so narrow that bounds the privilege and the treason, that

the faithful citizen is only able to meet the evil
when the traitor casts off disguise, and stands
forth at an armed advantage, to overturn the
State. Nothing but an immediate and overwhelming rally of loyal citizens can prevent a
transient victory for the disorganizers, if the
ramifications of the plot have been extended, the
precautions ample, and the *overt offence* be, at
last, sufficiently bold.

These are a few of the leading elements which
have borne a significant part in shaping the
present national issues. It would not be hazardous to predicate upon these those earlier disaffec-
tions which threatened the internal tranquillity
of the nation, but were quelled for the moment.
Even as to those, it is a question whether the
bold vindication of law by the Government did
not accomplish more than the contemporary
compromises, so called, and whether, had the
latter been wanting, we might not stand to-day
at a point far more advanced in social and political greatness, and be free from the peculiar issues
which, by those very compromises, were only
fostered, and thereby transmitted with an accumulated intensity and virulence of operation
and spirit.

V. Question of Slavery.

It would be violence to the subject not to
recognize the palpable fact that the elements of

political prostration and decay, already alluded to, have derived peculiar force and vitality from the presence and operation of the abnormal system of human slavery. Though the present generation is not responsible for its introduction, though the founders of the Republic deplored its existence and erected their temple of liberty upon foundations inconsistent with its perpetuity and expansion, and though, like all other systems of oppression and wrong, its doom is certain, it does, nevertheless, exist, and affect the entire social and political fabric of the State. Our past career proves, however, that the nation can prosper and advance, even under the weight of this burden; and that, with a genuine patriotism diffused through all hearts and sections, we can still labor earnestly and unitedly for the public weal. But it is equally true that, in States which entertain this domestic institution, the fundamental elements of discord, before adverted to, have had peculiar force and sanction. Timid in the presence of superior and controlling forces, indebted to the law of toleration, rather than that of nature or revelation, for its continuance and power, it cannot fail to be anti-democratic in essence, and aristocratic in manifestation and tone. Religion and true loyalty to country are indeed as purely and nobly cherished where slavery has its foothold as elsewhere; and when these hold in subjection to their redeeming and

2

ennobling work its operation and spirit, we may hope for an end to all our conflicts and its own extinction; but when the animus of human slavery becomes the absorbing sentiment of any ambitious clique or faction, and rules by its own inherent demands and necessities, the confusion of its advocates or the ruin of the nation are the sole alternatives.

I say this much, not by way of party logic, nor from failure to appreciate the virtue, self-denial, and patriotism of the South; nay, rather because, knowing these well in their purity and value, I behold their exponents silenced or over-shadowed by the more daring and unscrupulous manifestations of the turbulent and rebellious.

OUR PRESENT STATUS.

We have passed through a constitutional election of a Chief Magistrate of the United States. He received the electoral vote of a majority of the States, representing two-thirds of the population, material wealth, and physical power of the nation. Those States accept the Constitution as it is, and, further, avow their readiness to surrender all mere matters of construction to the authority having the matter in charge. They would go farther than this, and settle beyond reasonable cavil all parts of the organic law which need distinct explanation, if such there be, to render the whole more harmonious and complete.

The government, elected by the people, assumes the reins of power. In their charge are placed the care of the public property, the vindication of the public honor, the assurance of the public peace. Land, wherever situated, forts, however located, treasure, wherever deposited, belong to the entire people, and no section can, of right, arrogate a claim to any specific or distributive share, or legally alienate from the Federal centre its possession and control.

The obligation rests upon the government to protect each and every citizen, wherever located, from illegal arrest, and the destruction of his constitutional franchise and rights. If he be oppressed by few or many, it matters not. If he be imperilled, or overawed in attempted self-vindication of those rights by *organized* violators of the public peace, his claim for full and adequate redress is not impaired; but, on the contrary, it is increased in proportion as he loses all other methods of redress, and is forced to look to the central power for any possible relief. While, therefore, this government is powerless to usurp undelegated authority, it cannot shrink from that which it is sworn to exercise. It may, and should, exhaust peaceful and conciliatory measures with the offenders; it may adapt its policy, so far as practicable, to subdue excitement and ensure reflection on the part of the disappointed or rebellious; but it cannot extend such measures to abnegation of its own superiority without becoming, in time, traitor to the people and State. Acting under the Constitution of the United States, and bound by its provisions, the extent of any disaffection cannot change or impair the duty, but rather must enhance the responsibility, at least until by other and legitimate methods the existing relations of the parties shall be determined, or shall be predicated upon a new and different fundamental basis.

EXPEDIENCY AND SANCTION.

All questions of expediency and peaceful adjustment lose force and value as soon as they cease to operate as remedies for the evils threatened. The use of sanctions and the vindications of authority must then be interposed at the very risk of war itself; nay, war exists before a blow is struck, and the extent and nature of its manifestations must determine the appliances which shall be rallied for its arrest. I arrogate to myself no special office as teacher or guide; but as citizens, let us not prove blind to the issue that is upon us. While we have for days, and weeks, and months, plead for almost any relief from war, it is nevertheless true that a greater evil than war may befall us. I would that we could seriously appreciate our exact standpoint, and feel that we ought not, *must* not, simply look to our own individual concerns, as a State, or section, but remember that we stand responsible to millions, in the disaffected States as well as here at home, for the assurance to them of liberties now in peril.

With this general statement of the case, let me pass to consider very briefly our position as a nation, under the Constitution *as it is*, the nature and tendency of the disaffection as it exists, and our responsibility, whether willing or unwilling, for the perpetuation of that Constitution, and the liberty it secures.

OUR NATIONAL PRESTIGE.

Our national position is a proud and noble one. Of all the European struggles for liberty since our own Republic has held a place among the nations, not one has originated, advanced, or come to an issue, without a decided moral support from the United States. Its proud isolation from external attack, and its matured power and influence, have given shape to aspirations, and engendered hope of ultimate freedom, the world over. The policy of every maritime State has been liberalized, softened, and to a large extent modelled upon the assurance of our own expanding greatness upon the sea. Interior powers have learned to pay us the same respect. Our position, midway between civilized Europe and half-pagan Asia, has given us the *locus in quo*, by which, with corresponding physical power and training, we can command the trade of the world. The very treaties which now govern the commercial relations of European States in times of war, have been initiated by the bold declaration of a more enlightened policy by the United States. The surrender of the right of search, the immunity of the goods of neutrals, the abandonment by Denmark of her impositions upon the trade of the Baltic, the independence of the western continent from foreign control, have all grown out of our own just demands, our asserted power, and our commercial pre-eminence. The title of American citizen has become a credential of safety and honor, reverenced by struggling commons, respected by governing tyrants. Peace with America has become a desideratum, and threatened war with America would derange the finances, impair the prosperity, and imperil the peace of all nations. American discovery, American invention, American science, no less than American power, wealth, and liberty, have raised her to that fulcrum of force from which to move and direct the world. Fealty to our own boasted liberty, justice in dealing, and unswerving loyalty to principle, would secure us the title and influence of the model State.

THE CONTRAST.

No pen of mine, nor imagination of man, can portray the contrast, when dissolution, degradation, and cowardice shall characterize the once *United* States; when, torn to fragments, bereft of dignity and power, they shall become the prey of internal discord and foreign license. A failure in Hungary, with our example still bright and illustrious, is less a failure than a temporary check. A failure with us is signal, fatal, and universal. It cannot but relax the restraints of law, let loose the passions of the evil-minded, undermine the confidence of the good, threaten the integrity of personal rights and personal industry, and dissolve all political relations into anarchy and desolation, or breed some new combination; for, while that which is the fruit of willing compromise may live and prosper, as if no difference had once alienated the parties, that, which the majority yield to the mere force of intimidation and pressure, will prove the tunic of Nessus, fatal only to the betrayer of virtue and truth.

Such is our high position among the nations, and such the alternative with which we are threatened. What is our condition at home? We are even told that we must abandon the old Constitution, or perish. Rebellion, growing hourly, and with increasing violence and force, can indeed point to no liberties which the Union cannot preserve, no fundamental or practical franchise which the government of the Union will not secure. It demands a positive surrender

of Federal authority to the minority choice of a
restricted section of the country, or the issue of
civil conflict. It is not my design to ask by what
avenue this evil has thus matured and waxed
turbulent and daring. It is none the less pressing and actual, whatever its origin and growth.
It is enough for the honest man and patriot, the
man who loves liberty at the risk of offending
clique or party, that it exists, and that he has to
meet the duties it involves.

If the question were simply that of a willing
and legalized separation of free States, no matter
how my national pride might suffer, no matter
how much we should feel degraded among the
nations for such wilful surrender of our glorious
birthright at the behests of the institution which
would be the wedge of our separation, I, for one,
could trust Providence and the civilized world
with the reputation and destiny of twenty millions
of freemen.

THE PEOPLE DISCARDED.

But that issue, however and wherever mooted,
is not a practical issue in the matter that now
challenges our attention. The people at large
have adopted no authorized methods by which
even to consider the claims of so humiliating an
issue. More than that, I affirm that no man,
wherever he may live, and whatever part he may
bear in this struggle, can say with truth that a

single one of these thirty-four States has, by a legal and fair method, or by any method whatever, obtained the deliberate assent of its people to this rebellion. Not a single Court of Appeals, even in the seven extreme States, could fail to declare unconstitutional and void the acts even of its own disorganizing convention, upon a fair trial of its acts by its own fundamental law, independent of that of the United States. In no one State have a majority of the legal voters so expressed a choice. Even in Texas, the whole vote was comparatively limited and insignificant. In no single State was the so-called election of delegates permitted to reach the suffrages of the remote townships and common people. Of the choice of the remaining slave States, upon a free, untrammelled expression, I think no man can entertain a doubt. Even the wildest disunionist in the border States trembles lest the people shall be fully and freely heard. In Alabama, Georgia, Mississippi, Louisiana, and Texas, there are thousands who writhe under the swelling despotism, and only need a sure support to vindicate their rights. They need that protection which is their right and safeguard. Many who cry " hands off," *wish* peace ; but many, many more, ask for peace, only to rally the hosts of evil and ensure a more widespread desolation.

2*

FIRMNESS OUR ONLY SAFETY.

I ask, then, this simple question : Are we not impelled by highest duty to stand by the loyal and the true? Shall we despise their cry and neglect their liberation for fear of a contest with their oppressors ?

No man doubts that early and firm support would have given the Union men the control of every State. The tide grew only because it could grow unrestrained. If there had been no Constitution, no courts, no law, no process, no public sentiment, no religion, the usurpation could scarcely have been more steady, high-handed, and triumphant. No other government in the world could, with open, unrebuked treason in its legislative halls, have stood an hour, unless the traitors assumed of it, as they seem to have done, that it was respectable in mechanism, but, practically, fit only to be wound up quadrennially for the distribution of spoils and office.

Human wisdom trusted in peaceful measures, and if precaution and comity had gone hand in hand, all would have been well; but now the issue comes on apace, and nothing is left but vindication of authority. I would go to the extreme of honorable concession, but when concession aggravates rebellion, when its announcement is received as weakness, when the proffer of the hand is disdainfully rejected, and the hours of lenity are employed as a season of preparation for a fiercer conflict, concession becomes madness: it only aggravates the demands of the aggressor, and disheartens the real lover of honor and country.

To say nothing of public credit, national honor, and the vitality of the general issue, we are pressed to the point of the sword. Fort Sumter has been attacked and taken;* Fort Pickens may be stormed. But where does their change of occupants relieve the body politic? Since first their surrender was mooted, the times have changed, and to make the latter of these a voluntary precedent for similar withdrawals from other Federal soil, if it can now be held, at whatever risk, would be to bind the yoke upon the deserving and loyal of the South, and render their emancipation from that yoke the work of a more fearful struggle among themselves. Regarded separate and apart from the rights of the North, East, and West, in and to the waters of the Mississippi and the Gulf, and the unnumbered interests which are thereby inwrought into the very national fabric itself, can we do less for the South itself, in this exhibition of its own status, than vindicate law, assert authority, and leave the issue with the God of battles?

Such an issue, full as it is of sacrifice and hard-

* "Fort Sumter may fall" (as first delivered).

ship, is to be met with zeal and holy boldness. Better, far better, that we should be hurled into civil conflict than wilt under the scourge of a despotism more severe, and a treason more vile, than the world has ever witnessed. Tell me not that you would spare the flow of fraternal blood, and prefer rather the lash of the master and the sway of a despot. War, my countrymen, is indeed a vast evil; but there is a more fearful alternative, the surrender of our dearest birthright at the behest of despots and traitors.

If the legacy of the Fathers be no longer worth preservation; if law be a bugbear, and obedience a sham; if the State owe nothing to the people, and the people have nothing to expect of, or to render to, the State: what a mockery has our Union become, what a nuisance upon the face of the earth!

And yet, look at the elements which exist and would to-day triumphantly vindicate our honor if they could be brought into prompt and healthy exercise. Education is more general and Christianity is more diffused, in the United States, than elsewhere in the world. The principles of genuine liberty and the maxims of universal freedom are better understood, and more heartily cherished, in the United States than elsewhere in the world. The instrumentalities for their diffusion, the range of their influence, and the field for their application, are here pre-eminently displayed;

and the interests at stake, in their firm and perpetual establishment, are here more precious and multiform than elsewhere in the world. The moral power which underlies our institutions, if brought into exercise and made the inspiration of a just cause, would be invincible *against* the world. When our existence is threatened, as at present, *these* are the elements which should spring into the issue, and bend all parties and factions to their control.

And now to one more practical question before I dismiss the subject.

THE PRACTICAL ISSUE.

All the grievances of which the extreme violators of law complained before the people a few months ago, are ready of adjustment. No man dare deny it. What more would they have? Absolute, unqualified revolution! absolute, unqualified re-organization! There will even be found men before thirty days shall expire, and such there are now, if they dare avow their views—unless we burst from the chains that now fetter us, and rush to arms to vindicate our imperilled liberties and rights, and strike down all traitors, wherever found—I say, unless you do this, and do it *now*, there will be found men who would rather accept the code of the rebel league, their governing system, and their leaders, ignore the claims of the people and the heritage of the past, dissolve the government of the Fathers, and accept the counterfeit, than spend one ounce of treasure or risk one drop of blood to save the Constitution as it is. The Union, purchased at such a sacrifice, would be a hissing and a by-word, a foul and loathsome thing, which it were religion to trample on and annihilate. But, because there are always pests in society, desperate robbers and constitutional thieves, we do not despair of law and justice; neither because there may be traitors to Liberty and the State at our own hearthstones, will we *abandon* Liberty and the State. Rather let us stand by the Constitution as it is, meeting with warm hearts and hands those political brethren who, differing in non-essentials, are true to the fundamental code of our national being, and, at any risk, however trying, or any sacrifice, however costly, execute the law, protect the oppressed, vindicate our honor, and perpetuate the State.

We may shrink from the encounter; we may dread the issue; but no struggle for the right is *so* hazardous as its betrayal; no blood is so costly as that which strangles the coward's heart, rather than be spent for life and honor.

We are fast enough already to spend blood and treasure to seize the land of the stranger. Let us *now* see if we have the nerve to maintain *our own.*

Let me not be misunderstood. I advocate no special party tenet in this extremity. I would use all the appliances that sound patriotism and solid judgment can command; but we are at war. It is our own existence that is at stake. The shedding of blood is a mere contingency in the contest, neither commencing nor ending the struggle.

And what is life to liberty! What is the loss of life to the sacrifice of all we prize dear! When the day comes that merchandise and commerce, office and party, a venture for political change for the sake of the transfer of political power, and the matter of income and interest shall outweigh a high and holy devotion to country, and defile its shrine by their consecration as the God of America, let the earth lament and the land cry out, for, surely, the heaviest of God's judgments shall be upon the people.

But we shall not fail. The age, which is an age of struggle, will find America rooted to the cause of Freedom. The Government may wither for a time through the apathy of the people; the Union may be embarrassed, threatened, and apparently dissolved, through the time-serving and cowardly handling of the politician, the timidity of the press, or the uninterrupted sweep of high treason; but, though shame shall mantle the cheek, and we hide the head, as we style ourselves Americans, the remnant shall be faithful, and all our struggles, however fierce, and all our burdens, however vast, shall be as the refiner's fire, to purify the cause, and push on the career of genuine freedom to its ultimate supremacy.

The Hour which brings the Peril, already defines the Duty and the Deliverance.

We shall not abuse our trust. The exalted privilege of leading the nations will not lapse from our control. Be not deceived! The people, prone to peace, and dreading the inroad of red war more than Pestilence or Famine, are coming with calm and deliberate minds to that sublime but solemn conclusion, that they will offer their lives and fortunes, a free-will offering, upon the altar of Country, Liberty, and Independence. I hear the shackles of party clang as they are dashed upon the earth. I see the bonds part that bind the devotees of self and mammon. I see treasure offered without stint, or limit, to purchase back the rights imperilled. In the lull which follows the fall of Sumter I see the presage of a tempest! It will gather volume, and roll from the East and North and West until you shall rejoice in every sacrifice of treasure, and glory in every drop of blood expended for the public weal; for the whole continent shall be free, and the nations of the world shall pay you homage.

THE WAR: ITS NATURE AND PROSPECTS, ITS MORAL AND SOCIAL EVILS, AND ITS ULTIMATE RESULTS.

DELIVERED TO THE SOLDIERS OF INDIANA, AT INDI-
ANAPOLIS, IND., FEBRUARY 22, 1863, WHILE COLONEL
OF THE 18TH U.S. INFANTRY, COMMANDING THE POST.

SOLDIERS OF THE REPUBLIC!—I greet you, on this anniversary day, with fresh assurance that the memory of Washington retains its precious-ness and power. His offices and trials, his warn-ings and his counsels, not only survive his de-parture from the scenes of earth, but their vitality and force still energize the body politic and in-spire the people he established with the senti-ments of pure and substantial liberty. His panegyric is written in our every-day history. Observe its issues, and remember him.

True it is that the tide of civil prosperity which has borne the nation on to unexampled wealth and expansion since his departure seems checked by the crosses of an unexampled war. True it is that the citizen has left the furrow and the workshop, the desk and the office, for the issues of battle. True it is that war rages. From lake to gulf, from ocean to ocean, men arm to fight. A nation most free, a people most intelligent, a community most richly endowed with intellectual, religious, and physical virus, have directed the forum, the pulpit, and their exhaustless wealth of material power to the art of destroying life. *Invention* writhes for grander results, that it may vanquish or surpass results hitherto attained. Sea and land groan beneath the weight of monstrous engines, designed to overthrow the labor of the last. In proportion as modern skill had gathered up the agencies for that higher type of civil life inaugurated by the Fathers, so does modern art surpass herself in the supply of means to slay and waste.

Who are the people panoplied for the battle? What cause has called to arms a mighty nation? Why is treasure offered without stint, and blood without measure? Why does the father send forth his first-born, and his last-born, *then* follow *himself*, while mother and wife bid them all alike a hearty God-speed? *See!* All domestic ties relax their grasp, freely to surrender the loved ones to the embrace of the great destroyer! Marvellous spectacle in this advanced age of human progress! Strange tragedy, wherein a nation acts the parts, and the astonished world shrinks back from the real death which assails each character and fills each scene !

The people thus panoplied for battle are the citizens of the United States of America. They are *citizens*,—self-thinking, self-relying, self-governing citizens ! They are neither slaves, nor serfs, nor subjects, but co-equals in governing and educating the State. THEIR WILL IS LAW. Their law is the crystallization of their concurrent will. Their country is the matured fruit of many generations of self-denying toil. Blood has before watered the earth, that they might attain their present ability to war. The sacrifices of those generations have culminated in the gift of this wonderful faculty to destroy.

Their *country* has been the model and admiration of the world, and no less the terror of all who scorn and oppress the *citizen*. The centre, yes, the very heart of the new world yields this people life, and all its throbs so energize the body politic that each pulsation, more subtle than the electric flow, impels all other nations to a higher mode of life and culture.

THE OLD WORLD AND NEW.

You whom I now address are citizens as well as soldiers. You represent the *mind* as well as the muscle and the martial spirit of the nation ! Permit me, then, on this sacred day, to glance still again at the proportions of this surpassing

Commonwealth, and contrast it with other forms of civil life, that we may better appreciate its value, and may more courageously dare all sacrifices, to hasten that perpetuity which we feel and know to be ordained of Providence for the union of the States.

Its founders feared God! He blessed them! Their sons erected the sanctuary in their villages, and the altar by their hearth-stones. Wherever in the desert or far-off islands of the sea you find the word of God, and the praise of God, and their blessed fruit, wherever civilization is freshest, and human progress the best developed, you will find citizens of the United States. Go out over the world, if you please, to learn what you cannot learn of this people.

Behold columns, porticos, and temples, now in ruins,—ruins of the past. Will *they* develop man? There is no life nor real grandeur *there!* Behold the effete and time-worn dynasties that faintly imitate the prestige of barbaric times, now tottering under the pressure of the subjugated people, who yearn and toil and pant for their speedy overthrow! Do *they* develop man, *they*, whose sphere and fashion soon shall disappear before the onward march of man, to assume his rightful place upon the earth, as man?

What is Art in the old world but the childish fondling of old-time fiction or the mythology of the ancients! What is *science* in the old world but a spasmodic struggle to attain a higher sphere than the conditions of their civil life can justify! What is *religion* in the old world but the worship of the mysterious and the old, for mystery's sake, and because it is old! What is *invention* in the old world but a desperate endeavor to rival the progress of the new and keep in life the civil state which is already overshadowed by the new. What in the old world *is* old that does not find a fresher, better type in the institutions of the new? What in the old world is *new*, that has not been generated by some precious germ wafted across the waters *from* the new? What is there from all those nations to engraft upon a fresh and growing Commonwealth? What have they for your envy, what for your profit, beyond the instructive lessons their histories impart?

And yet, how precious are the memories of the Fathers! Noble souls were those, to rise even in the middle ages, above the level of their times, and breathe such holy fragrance upon the land that throughout the vales of Italy and of France, along the hill-sides of Switzerland and Germany, on the plains of Poland and of Hungary, and in unnumbered other lesser States, the tree of liberty sprang up and lived in the very teeth of frowning tyrants. Nay, more! Let us do honor to the long succession of hallowed names which, from the earliest date of the Christian epoch, maintained, in pure and glowing heat, the embers of the sacred fire, and preserved those precious leaves of the tree of life, and those holy laws of human conduct which made it possible, in after-times, for civil freedom to emerge and culminate with every passing age. It is *not* that other nations *could* not have sooner burst the bonds of feudal power to revivify the earth with the light of a pure, pervasive liberty, but that they *did* not; and that this *new* world was made of Heaven the *fulcrum* point, from which that liberty might work back upon the struggling nations of the old.

And thus it is that this people, now sublimely showing forth the greatness of their power and the terror of their outstretched arm, can bear the stress, and meet the issues here involved.

THE LOYAL ARE PROSPEROUS.

I said war rages! It is the great American Republic that is armed for battle. Even her children mimic war, and employ for toys the sword and drum and trumpet. And yet, with all the din of preparation—with all the munificence of expended treasure—with all the groaning arsenals replete with instruments of death—with all the array of marching columns and long extended fleets, what strange facts are patent to us all. The earth labors to outdo herself! The granaries burst with plenty. The husbandman has no need to garner up for future use, but yields his surfeit to other nations that are fed by this. The marts of trade are full of busy life! The loom hums on with undiminished zeal, and the steam-sped car, or ship, goes out and comes again, with ever expanding and multiplying profit. Surely, such a nation has no common mission to fulfil! Surely, this war now waged needs but a high and holy impulse to place this people on the pinnacle of the earth, a beacon light to all, the deliverer of all.

WHY THIS WAR.

Why, then, this war? I need not tread upon party issues. I simply recite such pregnant facts as point my lesson. It is the oft-told tale of *human struggle to be free.* It is the earnest that the citizen Republic will vindicate its origin in its perfected destiny. It is the daring venture of a great and mighty people to teach all nations how other nations failed, and, therein, to peril even the national life itself, upon the pledge, to make Freedom a fact, and Liberty a personal and universal experience.

The fundamental cause no man denies. The maxims of human pride, and the pretensions of the *few,* to make the law for *all,* which bound tight the chains about the patriots of earlier times, began to exact their claims upon the heritage of the Fathers. That which was abnormal and strange, in a *perfect* state, but was branded upon the national life at its very birth, began to usurp the functions of the State it lived upon. The exception, unfortunately induced, and unhappily transmitted, assumed to become the *law*, and to dictate the maxims of a Godless, cruel age to an age of Christian truth and liberty. Not content with the indulgence of the fundamental law which gave it tolerance, while anticipating its early end, this excrescence of human slavery assumed to mould the public shape in harmony with its own deformities. Exactions, consented to, assumed the tone and place of intrinsic rights. Resistance withheld, but tempered its appetite for new demands. As *its* portion of the national substance wasted, under its baleful creed, it coveted the richer portion of the Commonwealth, and cried, *give—give*—until the nation, heedless of all former distinctions of party or belief, cried out, with an united voice, " *Thus far, and no farther, shalt thou go.* Here shall thy proud waves be stayed."

Then came outspoken, bold, and defiant assertions of the true character of its mission, in a land of liberty, to *rule all* or *ruin all.* The Constitution, so long invoked as its protector, was derided and despised! Treason stalked in high places, and rude arms were stretched out to tear down the pillars of a nation's pride. What matter that the Republic outvied the world in power and glory! What matter that our commerce led all nations! What matter that, standing between both oceans, we held the keys of both oceans and the continents they laved! What matter that the world was fed at our hands, and that American invention had furnished the motive power of all human progress, and the vehicle for the electric flow of human thought! What matter that *here* was an asylum for the weary, worn-out exile from despotic climes; that *here Religion* had her altars; *Education* her throne; and *Purity* and *moral health* pervaded the civil and the social life!

All these (never so prosperous when freedom is suppressed) were so many galling proofs of the goodness and preciousness of the nation's life. *These, all these,* were living, breathing, speaking warnings to forbear. But, no! Even the presence of the nation's flag, the garb of the nation's soldier, the ermine of the nation's judge, the footsteps of a brother, coming from a State intact by the leprosy that was working in the vitals of the weaker and offended part, was as wormwood, to be cast out.

The vindication of authority, was miscalled force. The issue of legal process, was an usurpation upon vested rights. The protection of the nation's flag, and giving sustenance to the nation's soldier starving in a beleaguered fort, was considered *war* upon an independent State: until SUMTER—synonymous with the glory of our war for National Independence, and to be known in

8

future annals as the beacon spot from which
gleamed forth the fires of *universal* Liberty—
surrendered, but without disgrace. When, from
its ramparts, the flag of freedom disappeared,
Freedom herself mourned not! The earth, indeed, trembled as her sons rushed to arms! Such
power as no monarch ever boasted responded to
her cry! But *she*, rising to the clouds, took new
inspiration from the Infinite, as the good Angel
of Providence was permitted to unfold the issues
of the coming struggle. She beheld a nation,
loving peace, give up the sweet luxury of peace
to fight for truth and liberty. She saw the bonds
of party untwine and estranged brothers harmo-
nize for the public weal. She beheld armies
marshalled, battles lost and won, the faithful and
the faithless alike to fall upon the field of strife!
She beheld the sacrifice of noble souls and countless treasure! She heard the widow's wail and
the orphan's cry! She saw campaigns begun
and ended, and men's hearts to fail them, while
still they struggled on! She beheld new and
still newer sacrifices, hour by hour, and day by
day, through weary months or years, until a
nation, invincible against the world in arms,
seemed prostrate at the feet of the rebellious
few. She knew, full well, that Liberty must
surely triumph, and that every waste of life or
treasure would only prove the value of the prize
to be attained at last. And such *will* be the issue

of the war we wage. Faint not! Doubt not! Vast in expenditure, vast in its sacrifices, vast in its desolations, still more vast and over-shadowing in its results to the human race, will be this present, this expanding war.

A WORD TO THE PEOPLE.

Soldiers, were my voice to reach the people, I would say, *Statesmen*, you who love the Constitution of your Fathers, and the institutions they so dearly purchased, cheerfully labor with your counsels and your hands! *Partisans*, of whatever name, however you differ in minor points, gird up your loins for the final issue! *Citizens* of the great Republic, you whose power is the State, and whose will is the law of the State, dash away all doubts, for you again shall be citizens of a restored and undivided commonwealth. *Church* of *Christ*, praise God that you live in the culminating age of human progress, when your prayers and praises, your self-denials and your labors, but herald forth the coming day when Liberty and Religion shall govern the earth, and prophecy shall be eclipsed by the glories of glad fruition.

But that day has not dawned. You will be called to meet many grave responsibilities first. War, however just and holy, has its penalties. While, therefore, you fight on, for a generation if need be, to vanquish this unholy rebellion, you must not forget nor underestimate its tendencies and dangers.

Peace is the true destiny of the American people.

Your institutions are founded upon Peace. Your industry and your learning, your philosophy and your religion, all expand in times of peace, and dwarf amid the alarms of war. The social life will palsy, the currents of sin will course more freely, and the dangers to the commonwealth are then more serious, because their progress is overlooked or slighted amid the stirring pageants of a great and overshadowing war. Crime, that would shock the most hardened, stalks boldly forth! Vice, that would make of man an outcast, becomes too common for notice. Excitement breeds upon itself; and the unwonted stimulus of the public pulse draws new fever from every source that can intoxicate the mind. You *wonder, tolerate, pardon,* because it is a time of war. Now is the time for the good citizen and Christian to bestir himself, lest God in judgment shall protract the struggle. Because restraint is relaxed and rein is given to appetite, never withhold your zeal to conserve the interests of a peaceful life. You cannot, indeed, repress an excited pulse; you cannot stand still as the whirlwind wraps you in its folds; but you can do better: anticipate its coming, that you may give direction to the current and provide against its ravages. Strange as it may seem, your hearts, once so keen to sympathize with human sorrow, and so respectful to the passing bier, will grow callous, and your ear will deafen to the cry of human anguish. In the incessant call upon your patience and your pity, you will often doubt the merit of the suppliant, and turn away from the wail of the desolate. But rise to the merit of the pending struggle. Remember that you, as a people, are an example to the race. You, your sons, your brothers, and your friends, fight for *universal* Liberty. Your sacrifices are for *man*, *as man*, no less than for those who have gone forth to the battle.

THE RESULT CERTAIN.

Sublime and grand will be the history of this war, if, as now, with united prayers and energy, the whole people resolutely, faithfully, and in the face of no matter what disaster, still fight on. But, faith in great principles, assurance of glad issues, and anticipations of ultimate and conclusive triumphs, will not meet the obligations that belong to every-day life. This war, so holy, so inevitable, so indispensable, in the providence of God, to the elimination of the gold from the dross, and the establishment of a model civil State, has practical duties additional to those already referred to.

YOUR ENEMY.

You war with no common enemy. They are of your own blood, and they know how to fight. Because they fight to *destroy*, and you fight to *maintain*, the unity of the States, is no reason why they should shrink from your steel, or wilt as your flag flashes over your advancing columns. They have passed *that point*, and fight more desperately than in a holier cause. You peril much, but they not only peril all, but destroy all rather than your victory should find anything better than their lands and streams for your recovery. They gather old and young to feed the flame of battle. They waste and ruin! Yet they wither under the despotism they establish, and are even now on the verge of bankruptcy, utter and remorseless; while their rulers still drive them down the current.

This brings no joy to us; but when we feel our sinews stiffen, when we see the loyal States so prosperous, when we realize that in no great measure have we exercised our powers, we know that a swift, hearty, and united outpouring of the infinite resources at our command, by land and sea, would end the struggle, and restore the nation to a better and more enduring phase of civil life.

YOUR TRIALS AND DANGERS.

With all the general prosperity and thrift that surrounds and vivifies the loyal States, you should not forget, as soldiers or citizens, how many evils abound, nor how jealously you should guard your character and life. You must prove how a great Christian people can war, and yet rise above the contingencies of war. You must learn that you will endure and suffer, but that, therein, may be found your grandest victories.

Let me candidly speak of some of those evils, that we may meet them squarely face to face.

The Expenditure of Life not wasted.

And first: there must be great flow of human life! Youth, who are the sole representatives of names and households, will perish with them. Perish, did I say? No, never! Their blood shall invigorate the tree of liberty, and their comrades and friends will call them blessed. But there *will be* great flow of human life. The intelligent and gifted will fall, and their place must be filled by others. The sick, the wasted, and the down-broken will be so much prolific life lost to the body politic, and a generation will repeat the waste in unnumbered types and forms. All this will try you as a people.

Increase of Taxation a Test of your Patriotism.

Again. The burdens of civil life, in the support of the government you love, will press more heavily upon those who survive the issue of the war. Taxation will increase. The cost of your franchises will be enhanced, and your patriotism will be put to a sterling test. You may feel restless under new demands; for it is a law of your nature, and you cannot help it. You will be almost tempted to abuse the Providence which has jarred the even course of a peaceful life, and crossed your schemes of gain or comfort. But no change, based upon discontent, or a faltering love of country, under whatever sacrifices, can improve your lot. The government which claims your support is *your* government, and *its* interests are *yours.* Perfection of administration or policy belong not to man. Labor on steadfastly for the common good, and many years shall not pass by until every sacrifice shall be a theme of glad thanksgiving. Compare your civil blessings, under all these trials, with those of other nations, and you will find no weight of obligation too heavy for endurance, and no burden so vast that you cannot survive its pressure.

There will be Suffering.

Other burdens, no less weighty, will be added to those already referred to. Poverty and misery will come to many door-stones to plead for adequate relief. The widows, whose husbands have fallen ; the mothers, who have consecrated their sons to their country's cause, and who, sad and comfortless, bemoan their loss, will look for some practical test of the nation's estimate of the rights their sacrifices secured. It would be a burning shame, while any live in luxury, and have means to spare, that such as these should suffer, or have cause to regret the sacrifice endured. In the high tide of an excited public pulse sacrifice is light and easily endured. There is a pride in being recognized before the world as prompt to answer to the public call, which too often carries away the judgment and the brains. But when desolation comes to the lonely household—when the staff of support is broken—when penury creeps in at the windows, and no comforting friend treads upon the threshold, the lot is bitter and the home wretched. See, you, that no such homes abound, if your hand can extend relief. Food to the hungry, clothing to the naked, solace to the mourning, and the sweet balm of sympathy to the downcast and wasting, will turn their lot into a lot of blessing; and their hearts will rejoice in every drop of blood vouchsafed to preserve the nation's liberties. Kind words cost nothing ! They are a solace that no sorrowing heart rejects. They bless the recipient. They soften and humanize and ele-

vate the giver. They partake, in nature, of those
ministering spirits who soar above the earth to
bless the pure and holy in their sorrows and
their cares, and speed their flight, at last, to a
better land, where care and sorrow are no more.

Temptations of the Soldier.

But the increased weight of governmental
obligation, the waste of life, the increase of
poverty and domestic sorrows, are not the only
issues from this war that test your fitness to
transmit the inheritance of the fathers to those
who are to follow you. Already have I hinted
at a more melancholy result of the waste and
mischief of a protracted war.

War, which transforms the citizen into the
soldier, gives new scope and force to the human
passions. He who was an orderly, quiet man at
home, and who was loved for his goodness, gentleness, and grace, becomes, of necessity, inured
to deeds of daring and blood. He who was
reverent, sincere, and pure, is brought in contact
with the profane, the licentious, and the vile.
He whose highest pride was to deserve the favor
of his household, his neighbors, and his God, is
overwhelmed by the inevitable associations of the
camp; and, by the very force of continued pressure, is tempted to follow the lead of those who
scoff and deride the holy and the pure. He,
whose seat was never vacant in the house of

prayer, forgets there is a Sabbath. He, whose party or social fealty was but a synonyme with unconditioned patriotism and truth, too often takes up the law of license, and ignores the rights of all, if he but acquire the power. Accountability for his acts, as a soldier in the field, is recognized, because the law of his new life is inexorable and straight. But accountability for his social life is too often deferred until he shall return again to social life. He, who was sober, chaste, and temperate, takes up the social dram, becomes the prey of monsters in the human shape, degrades himself, destroys his better nature, and ruin is his portion.

Even here, surrounded by the associations of well-ordered, social life, how soon the enlisted man is tempted to put off the manners of the citizen, and don the independence of the soldier. They who have visited this Capital, at fair, festival, or party jubilee, now feel free to engage in pleasures which would have shocked their moral sense a year, or even a few months, ago. This is not strange. The soldier is habitually generous, sharing all things in common with the comrades of his mess; exposed to like dangers, and assimilated in daily habit by the identity of purpose and pursuit, they are no less one in all that relieves the routine of daily duty, and cheers the monotony of a garrison or campaign life.

You see a citizen staggering on the street, or

feel an offensive thrust, or become the object of
a sneer, a laugh, or insulting word, and you are
disgusted or incensed. But, to the soldier, you
involuntarily extend your charity and sympathy.
In *him*, it is treated as the explosion of a little
surplus spirit, which expends itself in objec-
tionable forms, but only lasts until the bugle
calls, or the drum recalls him to his post. The
citizen you look upon as ruined. You half pardon the soldier, and feel meanly if you take
offence. And let it be remembered, that the
mean and sordid do not go to war to risk their
lives for others, or others' rights. The prompt-
ings to the field have not the stimulus of fortune-
hunting, and few men enlist to better their pecu-
niary lot. The impulses that have filled the
ranks in the present war, have, for the most part,
been such as do honor to the human heart.
Heart-rending partings have been fewer; generous, free-hearted surrenders of loved ones to
their country's call, have been more abundant
than in any war since the sacred wars of Israel,
generations before the birth of Christ. And yet,
the elements of a free and open-handed nature,
no less prove the soldier's danger and the mag-
nitude of responsibility devolved upon every
citizen. A kind word may subdue the ruffled
temper. A sweet whisper of home may curb
the excited passion. A hearty assurance of
earnest wishes for his highest good may re-

establish the yielding spirit, and restore that trembling moral balance, which, once lost, is too often lost for ever.

You know, and I need not remind you, how one short year ago even the firm man of business dropped the tear of unexplained sympathy, when the first train of armed young men went forth to the untried field. You remember how they were followed with substantial tokens of your sympathy and respect! Are the fountains exhausted by that overflow? Are the sources of your plenty dried up by those generous benefactions? Or, rather, in your safe and quiet homes, have you become indifferent to their departure, and so familiarized with the steady tramp and the martial strains that you forget their dangers and their destiny when the battalions turn upon another street? There is homely truth in this belief. It takes a strong nature, thoroughly imbued with the grace and love of God, or with noble sympathies and a ceaseless flow of patriotism and love for your fellow-man, to maintain this protracted draft upon the human heart.

Have I colored the picture too highly? Nay, deepen the colors, intensify the outlines, and you shall never overestimate the sad tendencies of an extended, protracted war. It is easier to yield to a current of human pleasure than resolutely to stem it. To *yield* has the prestige, and is grateful to the natural heart. To *resist* requires philosophy, courage, principle. Many a youth has fought a gallant fight against his country's foes, who lacked the courage to control *himself*. Many a youth whose cheek once mantled at the ribald song, and who staggered, at the heaven-defying oath, has learned to hear with patience and without rebuke, if not to join the chorus, or repeat the oath. If such prove the tendencies of service in the field, what shall we say of their reflex influence upon the State. How strong is the impulse of the disabled, discharged, or deserted to re-live, in social and civil sphere, the form of life they led when free from their restraints. How strict the restraints of home and law must seem to those whose interior and external life alike (beyond the range of military rule) have been so different from the ethics of a well-balanced, peaceful State. But when thousands multiply by tens, and the million of men now clad in martial vestments shall return to the homestead and the ballot-box, how supremely wise and well-ordered must be the common-wealth which shall reassimilate their natures to its peaceful sphere, and soothe their redundant passions with the flow of overmastering goodness and moral force.

OUR NOBLE ARMY.

True it is that no army ever stood in battle so doubly armed with a cause so just. No country hitherto sent forth so many of her choicest sons to her defence. Never were so many of the good, the holy, and the pure, found battling with a nation's foes. Never did so many blessings attend, never did so many prayers follow an armed force, as have accompanied and followed the soldiers to this war. Thousands will return to enjoy with zest the luxuries of peace. The sanctuary will be thronged by kneeling forms blessing the God of battles, who hath given them their victory, and brought them out of all their troubles. But thousands more will gain no purification by the ordeal of arms, and society itself must be their restorer before they can again become her blessing.

A WORD TO PARTIES.

Keep, then, the social state alive with your most unselfish, earnest efforts. Let parties, which must always exist, and whose very variance is the balance-wheel to give steady motion to the civil mechanism that moves the State, base all their zeal upon the fundamental laws of righteousness and truth. Let learned and unlearned, all crafts and callings, combine to conserve those sacred laws which, under God's blessing, will make even of war a refining fire, as it is the most trying test of a people's liberty.

Undaunted by the future, hopeful of results, strive together while your brethren are in arms

to deepen respect for religion and for law. Let
the returning thousands be cheered by the con-
trasts, so that crime shall shrink before their
martial footsteps, and under your goodly offices
they shall rejoice in the fruit which the well-
nurtured tree of liberty so generously bestows
upon all who respect her laws.

And you, who are so exposed to temptation of
such varied forms, how shall I here warn you to
guard the beginnings of the evils that assail the
soldier's life ? Believe me, that vice is not made
honorable by its repetition or the number of its
votaries. A soldier swearing—and, alas, how
common !—presents the most fearful specimen
of this offence against good taste and the laws of
God. He, whose support alone protects him in
the field of strife, is insulted and defied. The
heart is hardened, the manner brutalized, and
the manhood degraded. You never knew a man
honestly proud of his proficiency in swearing.
Never try anything in which it is not a cause of pride
that you become expert. Keep your self-respect, and
you never will be a coward. Be chaste and temperate, and you will be sound and courageous.
In personal habits and every form of the interior
life of man, *as man*, adorn your character, as a
soldier, with all the best attributes of the peaceful,
genuine, honored citizen.

GENERAL ELEMENTS OF SOCIAL EVIL.

A great war tends to centralization of power, national arrogance, and the absorption of civil rights in the necessities of a military rule.

A war which directs the mechanical and industrial arts to its support, a war which, by its great expansion, appeals directly to the national love of ascendency over other nations, a war, like the present, which, while internal in its cause and operations, is nevertheless general in its physical effects upon the industry of all nations, is fraught with substantial dangers to the commonwealth itself.

In the first place, you become the object of widespread jealousy, if not hate. While good men and lovers of liberty the world over rejoice in all that develops liberty, it is far otherwise with those powerful dynasties which habitually suppress the gush of free instincts, and use the State for individual aggrandizement alone.

Your institutions invite assault. *Their very existence doubles the guard of half the continental powers.* Your living example speaks to all nations of a future for themselves. For nearly one hundred years the popular revolutions of the old world have found sympathy in the United States, and have been vitalized and refreshed by the assurance of your success. Within a single year your inventive genius has wellnigh disarmed the naval fleets of Britain and of France. They will *do* for *transports*. They may be reconstructed and adapted to *some* of the purposes of war. With most desperate energy the machine-shops and dock-yards of those great rival States are laboring, night and day, to make them useful in some such forms. That naval duel upon the waters of Hampton Roads, which sank the Cumberland and Congress, had wider range of scope and mischief than you at first supposed. *The balls of the Monitor which glanced from the walls of the Merrimac, penetrated the hulk of every European fleet.* The sloping sides of the Merrimac, which deflected the balls of the Monitor, at the same time resisted all projectiles that European skill had yet devised. The Merrimac, doomed in the charge of traitors, went to her own fate. The Monitor has also passed away, but her many consorts float on, the fear of traitors and the spectre to disturb the sleep of despots.

Europe flies to new expenditures of treasure to restore her naval power and prestige. But this involuntary tribute to your skill is not a gracious tribute. The admiration it inspires is not affectionate nor fraternal. It is the sentiment of the fencer or boxer, who finds his rival to be endowed with more cunning skill and more enduring muscle. He strives the more to improve himself that he may have better chance of future victory.

The leading European nations, constantly on a war basis, and wasting the bulk of their annual revenue in preparation for uncertain war; those nations, so faithless of their own position that they must prop up the State by a continual parade of armaments and arms; those nations, so suspicious of each other that continued peace is never the assurance of a new-year's birth, *are not, cannot be,* your sincere and disinterested friends. While you only advanced in the arts of peace and domestic virtue; while you fed them, clothed them, and supplied them with newly-invented arms and skilful forms of mechanism, of which you were slow to profit, they could easily endure you. Not so, when they must warp all their best resources from other channels to hold even pace with you in physical power and progress. Nor upon the sea alone has the descendant of the Puritan, the Cavalier, and the Huguenot equalled the modern European in the art of war. Nearly two millions of well-armed men have stood panoplied for battle upon American soil within a period less than half the duration of your last war with England. And, even that force, so vast, could be renewed, and still the nation would survive. Do those foreign States suspend their blows in the faint hope that the opposing sections will lash each other until they will become an easy prey, or too insignificant and feeble for fear or envy? How long will their affected forbearance last? And will not the unnumbered taunts they hurl, and the menaces they periodically repeat, stir up a spirit on this side the waters that will need firm restraint, if you would avoid the issue of a world-wide war?

True it is that a world-wide war may flow from the issues of this. The principles for which we contend have their leaven deep down in the organism of every social State, and ultimately must triumph in every State. But let us not hasten the general conflict, but wisely await our coming destiny.

DANGER FROM EXCESSIVE MILITARY DEVELOPMENT.

The attainment of military power, and the promise of military ascendency, develop in any people a strong tendency to use that power, and assert that ascendency over neighboring States, and to rush heedlessly into extended wars for selfish aggrandizement and glory. Military attainments, titles, and stations become fixed, and afford new avenues to place and power. Means are looked upon as ends, and this very military capacity, which should operate only as a subordinate instrumentality to insure security in the pursuits and habitudes of peace, is loved for itself and the honor it is supposed to impart. Of all lessons to be recognized and felt, the most difficult is this, that all force which society employs for its perpetuation or support, is identical and subsidiary, not paramount to, the civil interests of the State itself. Many a leader has started out, as did Rienzi, the last of the Roman Tribunes, with holy aims and patriotic zeal, who could not lay his armor down at the feet of the people, when the legitimate work was done, but has made of the people's confidence a throne to mount upon. *Not so*, WASHINGTON.

While the ability of a nation to defend itself is a substantial preventive against a needless war, its excessive development of a military taste is no less fraught with *incentives* to such a war.

As for the United States, it should be remembered that you have warded off attack when you had neither armies nor navies that would afford adequate defence. The best *defensive armor* of a just and mighty people *is their justice*. They stand serene amid the shock of arms, envied by all, respected by all. None wish to add them to their list of foes. All feel that the existence of such a State is large security to all against the assaults of each. Nations, armed to the verge of insolvency and ruin, pause before they hurl the gauntlet and wage battle for uncertain issues. And, besides this, so intermingled are the commercial relations of modern nations; so subtle are the laws of affinity, language, education, and religion, that already the world seems tacitly conformed to the idea that war must be the last resort. But for the fear of the people, and the emancipation of the people, armies would dissolve, and only a sufficient force would be maintained to insure respect and give force to the civil arm.

Ambitious men love power for power's sake, as often as to secure a higher stand-point for doing good; but America should never be the prize or plaything of such as these. Her fundamental law is the law of peace. Religion, the true basis of our institutions and our progress, teaches us her sweet lessons of peace. Her conquests are the purest and most complete, and the social fabric that rests upon her maxims will be immovable as the mountains, and its glory will pierce the heavens. Under peaceful sway the sanctuary and the school-house, the work-shop and the warehouse, the desk and the forum, and every type of human advancement, alike develop their intrinsic capacity to bless the nation and to work in full harmony with man's nature, and with a just adaptation to his better destiny.

To restore our country to such a peace, and in a new and more lasting union to draw fresh life from the institutions of the Fathers, we wage this war. The vastness of the outlay is only equalled by the priceless good to be attained. The sacrifices we endure, measured in the flight of coming years, will seem as nothing when compared with the mercies that shall be in store for us, if we push forward in the fear of God, meet

His requirements, and prove equal to our assigned position among the nations of the earth.

All this *waste of life*, these *financial burdens*, these *bereavements*, this *social disorder*, and their tendencies to ignore the normal laws that give the State its being and its value, will only prove the value of the State itself and purify its functions for a wider range of efficiency and blessing! Selfishness, or indifference, jealousies of party antagonism, may protract the struggle. New disasters may try your faith, and you may almost despair of safe deliverance out of these woes. You and I may not survive the struggle. Our fathers fought seven years for Liberty and Independence. You may be called of Providence to serve a double term of trial. Hecatombs of victims may be offered upon the same consecrated altars, and every household may wither as the blast of storm sweeps on; but in the day when men's hearts fail them, and desolation and barbarism seem to dawn upon this most blessed age for man to live and labor in, the remnant shall be faithful and they shall find a sure deliverance.

Go out, then, and take courage. Bind up the wounds of the bleeding; comfort the fatherless and the widow; pour the oil of gladness upon the sick and wasting heart. Deal gently with the erring. Cast him not off an outcast! Remember how much he has suffered, how much he has been tempted. Remember the absent soldier! He fights and bleeds for you! This is no sentimental fiction. *His arm has kept your firesides intact of the enemy. Your fields have not been swept by fire or consuming armies. Your lands are not exhausted of their products.* Your rivers are not closed to commerce, nor your shops to the busy life of trade. Your sanctuaries are open. Your Sabbath is sacred. Your halls of learning are only closed that their votaries may give their energies to the great struggle.

Thank God, and move on! True, you have no great and boasting allies to share the task you have commenced; but, by the memory of the Fathers, whose spirits hover in the air, to bless your last great struggle for independence and the rights of man, move on! True; blood flows; treasure disappears; moaning and wailing abound in the land; but, *blood it was that redeemed man, and by blood shall the nation be purified and exalted to her rightful place among the nations.*

INDIANA.

If I have said anything to inspire the tempted soldier with new sentiments of self-respect, to stimulate his pride of country and his courage, in this great battle for freedom, I shall be content. All this seems superfluous to Indiana troops. If I were disposed to commend you, I could say, that although a stranger here, six months ago, I am already knit to you by many grateful ties. INDIANA! where else is there so much just pride in those who have left their native State to battle for the Commonwealth! INDIANA! where else have legions sprang forth so promptly at each successive call! INDIANA! where else has a name become a synonyme of VICTORY!

Is it where the mistress of waters spreads wide her robes to greet the waters of the gulf? Is it upon some narrow island on the coast, where floods and tempests have wellnigh submerged the valiant band, or, where, floating across the adjoining waters, an island fortress is to be stormed and captured? BURNSIDE, son of Indiana, pauses amid the tempest, and smiles amid the flight of unnumbered bullets to greet his Indiana boys, and bid them on to conquest! Is it before the walls of *Yorktown* or the heights of *Richmond;* at *Sharpsburg, Manassas,* or *Antietam;* at *Rich Mountain, Carnifax,* or *Cumberland;* at *Columbus, Donelson,* or *Shiloh?* Ah! yes; it is *there,* everywhere! *East, West, North, South!* Wherever Indiana sends forth her sons at all, she sends them forth to fight and conquer. Her banners are shattered and ragged! Her battalions are thinned out and wasted! Her name, which is legion, is everywhere resounded, yet never will retreat or dishonor.

But I am not here, now, to congratulate Indiana. She has done well, and deserves more than I can render.

4

I talk to you to-day upon sad and solemn themes. Overwhelming responsibilities are on us as a nation. Unexampled sacrifices have been, and will be our lot. We shall pass through narrow straits, where overhanging dangers promise ruin on either side. But *look*—He who notes the sparrow's fall; He who cares for the minutest organism that deep down in the caverns of the earth has had its life and its enjoyment; He who guides the path, and guards the destiny of the minutest created thing that floats in the water-drop, or peoples the air we breathe as truly as He wheels the universe of worlds in their appointed course, has never failed, and will never fail, to bless the highest order of created things —*Man*—in His own image born, when he boldly pursues the path that leads to virtue, truth, and liberty.

I see, coming, foretold by *Him* who cannot lie, a time of Peace; and, still beyond, a time of *unexampled peace* and righteousness! The earth, so long the stage where every unholy passion has been expressed, and where the ravages of sin have made a charnel house of Paradise, and of this round orb, once shaped for the blissful residence of an unsinful race, a spot for angels to look upon with tears of pain and pity, shall be redeemed. The price, most precious, has been paid! War shall put off her vestments, and convert her means of torture to the happy uses of a perpetual peace. *Peace* shall multiply her mercies, until the earth shall wonder that her reign has not always been a universal reign. Joy and gladness shall fill each beating heart, and *man* shall appear again, as in the Eden of the past, the companion of his Creator and the Angels. There shall be music then. Banners shall float from every hill-top, and wave over the heads of the blessed; but the music shall be the outburst of pure and happy hearts, and the banners that wave over that restored and ransomed people, shall be the banners of an unwasting and perpetual love.

One word more before I close. I have spoken of this war in its *extent,* its *dangers,* its *sacrifices,* and its *future.* I have glanced at your position as a nation among the nations, and your illimitable resources for good to the race. I have drawn upon that distant future for the glorious issues that shall flow from all these present ills. I was tempted to pause, and draw a picture of the nation *at the feet of the rebellious States,* and see how *that vision* would meet *your favor and support.* What a spectacle that would be! The Mississippi closed at any whim of a hostile power; the Ohio lined with forts and alive with fleets; the border, a chain of custom-posts, and *you* indebted to a *foreign* State for leave to travel to the Gulf; an ever-widening breach of interests and aims; doubled armies, and ever-increasing cost, that you might not become the prey of sudden inroads or unprovoked assaults; the Gulf, itself, an inland sea, in another's grasp, to cut you off from the Pacific and its infinite range of wealth and power; the natural outlets of your commerce the sport of any who should chance to take offence at your principles or your polity! But no! The absurdities of anything less than a straightforward fight to restore the Union of the Fathers, at any cost, is never dreamed of, except in the brains of those who, having nothing to gain of a free and united people, would risk your ruin to make some capital of your dissensions or your fall.

SOLDIERS! *Citizens!!* you know *no such word as fail! You know no such article as disunion! It has no market here at any price!*

LEXINGTON and BUNKER HILL belong to INDIANA! YORKTOWN and NEW ORLEANS belong to INDIANA. You will cherish them, and cherish them for ever! You will not deal tenderly with the burglar while he assails your throat! You will not buy your own peace, if he will only take your family and your all! They, who have ruthlessly assailed the nation's life, will not find *you* more facile and placable, until they renounce their arms and return with penitence and new allegiance to the once honored union of their love.

I close. God Almighty fights for those who

fight for Him. If it be for His glory, and the glory of the race; if it be the spirit of His teachings and His law; if it be the choice of angels and the spirits of the blest; if it be the prayer of the Fathers who bend down from heaven to mark the issue of this war; of Washington himself; that a thorough and pervasive civil liberty, a pure and life-imparting Christianity, a general and well-diffused intelligence, the cultivation of the highest type of manhood through the head and through the heart, shall perish, and the world recede for centuries, to be restored only through new sacrifices and oceans of blood; then, and not till then, will you fail in this struggle.

You will fight on. Be true to your flag! You fight for liberty. You will triumph.

Then, when the war shall be over, there shall be no household in the land of which it shall be said, with the finger pointed, that its name was not represented in the great war for Independence; and no cheek shall tingle with shame when it be said his name is borne on no battle roll; but at every even-tide, in every home and hamlet, there shall be joy and glad thanksgiving, that to *it, in part,* belongs the Restoration of American Liberty and the Deliverance of Man.

KIND WORDS TO COLORED CITIZENS UPON THE RELIGIOUS, EDUCATIONAL, SOCIAL, AND PERSONAL DUTY OF THEIR RACE.

DELIVERED AT THE DEDICATION OF A CHURCH EDIFICE FOR COLORED CITIZENS, WHILE TEMPORARILY ON DUTY AT INDIANAPOLIS, JUNE 17, 1869.

In accordance with the desire of these colored citizens who are erecting a new house for Divine worship, and who believe that a few words of counsel from me will aid the enterprise and stimulate their aspiration to grow strong, in all the elements which give value to personal character, I have so far departed from a settled repugnance to speak publicly upon any subject, since the war, as to consent to this familiar talk upon themes that press immediately upon your condition and your prospects for the future.

My profession, as you know, does not occupy, nor aspire to occupy, the field of party politics or general oratory; and yet no calling whatever, can entirely absolve any Christian man from the ever present obligation to use influence and strength, at all proper times, in giving impulse and sanction to such moral and religious agencies as are material to the well-being and advancement of others.

I can well see that to the colored people of the United States the present is a transition period of great importance. It is a period wherein they have much to learn and much to do. Upon the spirit, courage, ambition, and purity of motive with which they labor, will largely depend the public estimate of their fitness for enlarged franchises; and, on the other hand, it is certain that if they accept national blessings with passive indifference, they will go backward, instead of forward, in all essential elements of civilized growth and culture.

There have been recent statements in the public press that in some parts of the South, where the restraints of the former social condition have passed away, there has been a partial revival of superstitions and usages which are essentially grovelling, brutish, and heathenish. While you cannot but regret, with others, any such tendency, it is no less certain that some such reaction was natural, and that there is laid upon you, and upon the whole American people, peculiar obligations at times like the present. You have, at home, in the midst of an advanced civilization, the more cause to make your whole life conform to the highest rules of moral action, in proportion as you enjoy privileges and mercies which those just freed do not possess, and can only gradually attain. You know that the arm is strengthened by exercise, and is weakened by disuse. The blacksmith's muscles are hard and tough as his sinews. The student and the idler—the one from exclusive brain-work, and the other from no work at all—are useless for almost all physical endeavor. So with many of your race. They need the *exercise* of the best qualities of manhood, and they need advice and encouragement from others in order that the large number just emerging from the pit of slavery may find support and countenance from the conduct and good behavior of their brethren who have enjoyed the blessing of freedom for years. There are few fields for the missionary and philanthropist where more good can be done than among the colored people of the South ; and I have undertaken this address to-night because I feel that you should not depend alone upon your own counsels, but seek from those who have had more learning and experience all possible help in the improvement of your race. I know that the clergy of this city, not of your color, are interested in your welfare, and that you will gain strength, knowledge, and wisdom by occasionally inviting them to your pulpits, and by gradual growth into their habits of life and thought.

I speak plainly and familiarly, hoping to quicken

4*

your desire, your industry, and your faith in the dawning future.

I shall not treat of education (as has been announced) in the common acceptation of that term.   The word is from the Latin language, and one part means *leader*, and was applied to great generals or commanders.   The word " education" might almost literally be rendered in English thus : " To lead out from ignorance, and establish the life of knowledge, happiness, and safety." When you are *led out* from temptation, you are being educated for a better life.   *As* you are *led out* from ignorance, so you acquire knowledge. Schools and books are not entirely within brick walls and muslin binding.   The whole world is a school-house ; every fact in daily life is designed as a lesson ; and all Nature is a book of study in the progress of education.

The end of American slavery has brought upon your race, which so long suffered under its fearful oppression, new responsibilities and duties.   That rescue has been so recent, that you hardly realize the fact and do not yet understand fully how to turn to the best advantage the freedom attained.

Many here present can remember years of struggle, during which the best of Christian ministers endangered life by advocating emancipation, and when the only channel through which benevolence could liberate the black man from slavery was to secure his exportation to Africa, there to begin life anew. I remember very well that thirty years ago the Rev. Noah Porter, at Farmington, Connecticut, had the windows of his lecture-room stoned, because of prayer for the slaves captured on the Armistead, who were being cared for on a farm near the village. And in 1849, when Frederick Douglass attempted to speak at the Ohio State House, fire engines were brought to the ground, to drown out the audience. And yet times changed so rapidly that, in 1861, I had the pleasure of delivering a flag to Mr. Langston, for the 58th Massachusetts Regiment (perhaps the first flag so presented), from the terrace of the new State House, near where Mr. Douglass had been mobbed.

The cowardice of State and Church had alike protracted the torture of the black race, multiplied the horrors of the dungeon, the lash, and the halter, and trained up a blood-hound class of leaders as merciless as the trained dogs of the Southern planters.

Year by year the nation increased its debt to justice and humanity, until God, in His mercy, instead of sending fire from heaven, as He did to consume Sodom and Gomorrah, only sent the greatest war of human history, and in the blood of a million of men, in the wasting of half a nation, in the tears and groans of countless widows and orphans, wiped out that generation of slave owners and redeemed a race to liberty.

If ever a curse came home to plague its inventors, it was slavery. The inventor of the guillotine is said to have had his own head cut off by his own ingenious machine. So, blazing cities, burning mansions, prostrate industry, and desolated plantations, felt the wrath of God through the march of the once despised Abolitionist. As if to make the justice more signal, exquisite, and complete, the "colored troops fought bravely," and, with arms in their hands, marched side by side with their co-deliverers to the enfranchisement of their people and the rescue of the imperilled Republic.

The boasted liberty which had taken refuge from the tyranny of Great Britain, and, embarking on the Mayflower, had landed in New England, thence to overrun a continent and become the light of the world, had fattened itself upon human blood and become the agent of the vilest outrages upon man. It was righteous and just that, in the sequel, Northern blood should also be spilled; for Northern timidity, avarice, and forgetfulness of the God who had delivered them from their oppression through the war of the Revolution, had hardened their hearts, and they refused to let the people go free.

As if to assimilate to the example of the children of Israel who, when they were hurried out of bondage, took the jewels and treasures of their task-masters, so houses and lands, and all the supplies of the Freedman's Bureau that were taken from the oppressors, were converted into blessings to aid and comfort the ransomed. The scourge of human slavery had so long sounded in the land that the Hand of High Heaven turned it upon North and South alike, and the wail over the death of the first-born was heard in every house, as years before it appealed in vain from the cabin and the negro quarters. Serfdom had ceased, though Slavery lingered. England and France had advanced in the right direction ; but America kicked against the pricks, and would not hear the voice of Providence or the groan of the sufferers.

Before the fall of Fort Sumter, in April, 1861, in words to the people of Ohio, and before blood was shed, I was impelled to declare this sentiment :

" We are at war. It is our existence that is at stake. The shedding of blood is a mere contingency in the contest, neither commencing nor ending the struggle. We shall not fail, for the age, which is an age of struggle, will find America rooted to the cause of Freedom. We shall not abuse our trust. The exalted privilege of leading the nations will not lapse from our control. Be not deceived. The people, born to peace, and dreading the inroad of red war more than pestilence and famine, are coming with calm and deliberate minds to that sublime but solemn conclusion that they will offer their lives and fortunes, as a free-will offering, upon the altar of country, liberty, and independence. I hear the shackles of party clang as they are dashed to the earth. I see the bonds part that bind the devotees of self and mammon. I see treasure offered without stint or limit to purchase back the rights imperilled. I see the presage of a tempest. It will gather volume, and roll from the East and North and West, until you shall rejoice in every sacrifice of treasure, and glory in every drop of blood expended for the public weal, for the whole continent shall be free, and the nations of the world shall pay you homage."

Fort Sumter fell! The rest you know. Had I declared a dream? The countless thousands of fresh blossoms that so lately exhaled their grateful odors from tens of thousands of honored graves are fresh testimony that I did not then, as one never can, overestimate the grandeur, the scope, the sacrifices, and the issues of that struggle.

The war came, was prosecuted and ended, and with it came the end of human slavery. Slowly but surely, the bad blood that remains is being purified by the application of beneficent laws and the persuasion of the necessary constraint, so that no long period will elapse before reconstructed States shall involve regenerated hearts, and the whole nation shall prosper and flower in the luxuriance of a better life.

Neither have I recalled the past and brought back bitter memories, with the purpose of stirring your passions, or unworthily triumphing over misguided countrymen, enemies in arms, but again to be brethren at heart.

The South is rescued from her worst enemy. Capital and manufactures and emigration are to build up her bulwarks as never could have been realized in that former unnatural life. Weights are cast off, and she runs with the North an even race of peaceful industry, in which each section shall rejoice and glory in the triumphs of the other, and find in the other the complement of itself, together, to make the " unit," our common country.

The colored people of the United States should look upon the past as the rescued mariner re-lives the sufferings he experienced when floating helpless upon a sea of unknown peril, that he may find new and more abundant cause for gratitude to the Giver of all mercy, and be better fitted for the realities of life.

The white man should often look back upon his career of power and its wrongful uses, to learn how much he owes to a race that so long suffered at his hands.

Hear what I have now to say, with an earnest purpose to so live that you will convince the world that you are worthy of freedom, and worthy of a country which not long hence will know no limit to human privilege but the perpetual obligation to do right and deserve God's blessing.

You have different capacities, tastes, and employments. You have many chambers in your brain, like the rooms of a house. All should be occupied by the right tenants. *Hate* must be *expelled* and *Love* must be *admitted.* All must work in harmony, so as to secure the best results in every phase of daily life.

YOUR RELIGIOUS LIFE.

This is fundamental and will shape all life. Not alone in the free Northern States, but while chained to the wheels of Southern capital and power, it has been a peculiarity of your race, that respect for *some* religion has been almost instinct and constant. If, for want of other friends, a sense of dependence upon the Creator drove any to that love of religious worship which became so characteristic, it was certainly very natural; but behind that was another fact, accepted as true by most African travellers, and the best writers upon the character of the race. The African, even when heathen, is enthusiastic in his devotion to some Supreme Being whom he accepts as the source of life and blessing. His thoroughly innate capacity for music finds the highest themes for jubilant praise and melodious chorus, in worship. However restricted in sentiment, or novel in execution, there is an overflow of zeal and genuine gladness which indicates some melody of soul. The Mississippi steamer, the plantation, the cabin, and the forest have resounded with his songs, when all that he seemed to possess, to give thanks for, was mere life and the chance of its continuance. Whether trudging to the cotton-fields, grinding the cane, or driving his team, the ever-jubilant refrain told of his capacity for happiness, and how keen were his susceptibilities to enjoy.

Few scenes were more full of wild and thrilling interest than a visit to some colored church at the South on the Sabbath, when a great assembly, relieved from the pressure of week-day duty, made the very walls tremble with the volume of their song, and when a strange delight and delirium of gladness in the worship of the Great Master, seemed almost to separate soul from body, and take the spirit into the presence of the Invisible. This religious feeling has not abated with the rescue of the race; but, with the increased latitude for its indulgence, there must be a wise direction given to its fervor, in order that it may prove a genuine element in elevating and purifying life. It must be refined, methodized and instructed, through intelligence and wise counsels. Other conditions of life, pre-eminently that of systematic labor, must be allied with *it*, and this is to be accomplished only

through your own improvement and corresponding effort to improve others.

Your Sabbath-schools vie with any in their
outward prosperity, and the generation which is
now coming to maturity, untrammelled by the
sneers, the contumely, and abuse of other races,
can look up and around, and as you address the
Creator of all things as *your* God, so you can
shout and sing,

> " *My* country, 'tis of thee,
> Sweet land of Liberty,
> Of thee I sing."

Well was it for your race while in bondage,
that, instead of simply grovelling like the cowed
brute under the lash of oppression, there was
music in your nature that buoyed up your soul
and gave you access to the Throne.   To be an
African was to be at least a natural musician,
and but for that ever-present agency, the power
to sing, how could the race have been saved from
blindness and degradation too deep and utter to
have been rescued for generations?

Wisely do you cultivate that faculty.   *It is
hard to find a spontaneous, cheerful singer, who is
either wholly rogue or brute.*   Where song flows as
the stream, from a constant fountain, there is
almost always affection, fraternity, and reverence.
It has been the outlet for the joy of worshippers
through all ages, and it is the glory of countless

angels and archangels about the great White Throne. It is the happiest outflowing demonstration of purity of heart, and it rises like grateful incense to the Author of all that blesses man, upward, to that God who has given to the rustling leaves, as well as to the birds, a share in the ceaseless song of Nature, and whose entire universe is full of melody in sweet accord with His matchless love.

The stoniest heart is reached by music. Cultivate it for yourselves and your families, and when the hour shall come in which to dedicate your new sanctuary to the service of Almighty God, let not praise alone abound, but make it a sacred temple, from which, with a truly consecrated life, you may go forth into the world, and as men see your good works they shall know and testify that you walk with God.

Shouting and *singing* are not all of *religion*, but when your music flows from the joy of a peaceful spirit and a consistent, pure, and useful life, you may rejoice that you can sing, and may well sing as you rejoice.

INTELLECTUAL LIFE.

Next, and handmaid to religion, and essential to an intelligent view of religious obligation and duty, in the peculiar position of your race is the acquisition of knowledge. There are old and gray-headed men and women among you, and some of them may not live to see the completion of your new church edifice. How painfully have the slow years dragged, as they waited for the Year of Jubilee! How has faith wavered, and how has it seemed as if the right hand of Jehovah was shortened, that it could not save, until, when deliverance comes as on the wings of the morning, they can almost say with Holy Simei, of old, " Lord, now lettest thy servant depart in peace, for mine eyes have seen thy salvation !"

They were youth when—to strive to read—was to suffer. You, their children and grandchildren, no longer a despised race, but maturing in the work and franchise of freemen, have great inducement to bring every child and youth into the speediest and best cultivation of the head as well as the heart. *Lead out* every good faculty you possess. Help educate yourselves. France has repeatedly given the honors of her National Academy to the colored man. The President of the United States has acted in the spirit of the American people, by introducing worthy men of your color into places of trust and honor. The ship yards and printing offices of the United States no longer make complexion a test of fitness. Moral progress is ever onward and upward. There is no back-track for a revolution against iniquity. They who do not see the advance of Right are the greatest sufferers, whatever their profession, trade, or calling. To be deemed worthy as any, you must deserve as well as any. It matters not what may be your occupation, so that it be honest and useful; but it does concern you that you acquire knowledge, that you read the history of your country, that you read of its past so thoroughly as to understand the demands of the future, and that every child shall be early taught the principles involved in a fair common-school education, and thus be able intelligently and successfully to keep an even way with those who for generations have been in your advance. Thus, and thus only, through this constant effort at self-improvement, will your field of influence enlarge, so that your people will command respect, and you will be able, in turn, to assist in the development and improvement of those hundreds of thousands at the South who have not had the privileges which you enjoy.

Thus will you lay the foundation for filling your pulpits with well-read and successful preachers of the gospel. It will not answer that they have simply the fervor of warm hearts. They must, with you, and more than you, cultivate the *head*, as well as the *heart*. Thus also will lawyers and physicians spring from your midst, who will honor noble professions. Thus will you rise to the platform of true manhood, and the finger of scorn will only rest upon the ignorant and unworthy, whether black or white.

POLITICAL LIFE.

The embers that now and then flash in the extinguishment of the rebellion will soon be as dead as the ashes about them. Sooner or later you will go to the polls, and as you now pay taxes, so will you take part in selecting the men who collect and disburse those taxes. As there were those who denied in 1860 and in the spring of 1861 that a war was coming: as there were men who had no faith in its success and the hastening end of slavery, so there may possibly be those who will not see the position you are to occupy as men.

Temporary opposition and the discussion of its prudence or safety cannot long delay the consummation, if you are faithful to manhood, and be careful to deserve that which the nation tenders. Prepare yourselves for the coming duty. Nearly every institution of vice in the land retains life, only because honest, patriotic, and Christian voters do not unite for the best men and the best cause. Your votes will be wanted by everybody. You will find before long that you are thought a great deal of, and will be surprised how suddenly the idea came to light. Become fully Americanized; that is, identify yourselves with the welfare of the entire people. Inspired by religion, endowed by education with the discrimination you require, come squarely up to the standard of earnest, honest, and independent freemen, and your country shall have cause to be proud of you, as you will be proud of your country.

Already you have your color in the army. No American officer need feel ashamed to own himself " an officer of a colored regiment." Colored regiments meet their duty on the plains, or elsewhere, with credit to themselves and the nation. Clad in the panoply of right, fill up the measure of recurring daily duty, so that when you vote for the first time, and have a country in fact, you may feel like shouting, as I trust you may, when you exchange an earthly home for the heavenly, " *home at last !*"

I am no politician, and seek none of its notoriety or honors. I assume a fact which I know to be assured; and, as a fellow-man, I give you counsel upon principles of life and conduct, which, being those of Christian manhood, predicated upon the laws of God, govern us all, whatever our calling or color; and I speak under the conviction, that had I declined to meet you in the spirit of your assurance that my work would do you good, I would be unworthy my profession and my citizenship.

YOUR PERSONAL AND SOCIAL LIFE.

It is possible, my friends, for a freeman to be an educated, Christian man, and still to lack many qualities of person, or habitudes of life, that impart completeness to character, and distinguish an eminently useful life.

Good manners, neatness, and the outward refinement of the gentleman are by no means to be despised or neglected. As a people you have some natural aptitudes for other social qualities besides that comprehended in taste for music. The white man has, in fact, made money from crowded houses for years, by calling many most pathetic, joyous, or spirited airs " *Ethiopian Melodies*," and has complimented you thereby. If he borrows or imitates your music, see to it, that in your imitations from him, you select only that which is refined in manners and inures to your radical and permanent improvement.

A clean, tidy cabin, however humble, if suited to your means, can be a home that will speak to every passing stranger of thrift, taste, and happiness.

We have abundant social feeling, and no people are more addicted to those neighborly reunions which develop the impulse of mutual support in affliction no less than that of sympathy in all rational and substantial pleasures.

Home is the first place to make happy. Let the gambling den, and all indulgence that wastes time, energy, or money, without imparting support or happiness to your family, or benefit to your head or heart, be shunned as you would shun a viper. Slavery of the body and soul to vicious indulgence is worse than the slavery from which your race has been redeemed by blood. It is the immediate curse of this nation, and a heavier burden to bear than the national debt, that physical indulgence and extravagance generally are dulling moral perception, and running the people after that which satisfieth not.

But, my friends, the best personal and social life involves labor. *Work is the law of our being.* All work will not be alike in worldly dignity or income. Life, in every sphere, has its methods and values; but the obligation of labor is ever present. Nature gives her examples. From the bursting seed, ambitious to come out to the air and breathe life with us, to the forest tree which by slow struggle has attained a power to resist the tornado and put to fault all human resistance, there is still found this law of patient, earnest work. If you look for a man whom you would trust, it is *not* the *corner-loafer;* but it is *that* man who, day by day, has something honest to do, and does it perseveringly, and, therefore, does it well. Women work; and in the sphere of home they toil with a faithfulness and devotion that does not alone impart to the life of man its solace and consolation; but when the care and culture of children have had their due attention, woman, by her intuitive perception, comes in with her counsels to strengthen and fortify man for duty, just as her gentleness, trust, and love make of

5

home a heaven in contrast with the turmoil of out-door life.

Life, as a rule, is all work. Pleasure is but a style of rest to body or brain, and is the balm which soothes the strain of labor, and not only refreshes the worker, but gives new zest to the work itself. Therefore, man and woman, rejoice in your ability to work. The drone of a hive must die. So the idle man or woman starves, and no willing companion is found to give refreshment earned by the toil of others. The old proverb, that "man is the architect of his own fortunes," is a good one. Buildings do not grow, as does the mushroom, in the night, to be given to man in the morning, without labor. Even the mushroom worked, though man did not help it grow, and though he slept while it labored. The problem is simple, and the humblest have their appropriate field of labor. The whole law of human progress is embodied in the question of personal respectability and individual duty.

A symmetrical life is not one which has placidly and evenly developed, undisturbed by, or indifferent to, its surroundings, but one that has surmounted obstacles, and has realized completeness through struggle and victory.

I have seen plaster casts that at first seemed true to the original marble statue which they were designed to imitate. How differently were they fashioned! The copy could have been made by any common worker, without the expenditure of much brains or genius. The original has been cut from the stone itself, by countless thousands of strokes, and when the earnest worker underwent wellnigh infinite anxiety lest in delicacy of touch, perfection of outline, or development of expression, contour or feature, he should so fail, that the failure would be signal and complete.

Thus, a well-developed, perfect life, has felt the chisel and hammer, and has attained completeness, not by the passive acceptance of a compress into some established mould, which was only mechanical and without the ethereal spirit to give to the result the highest success, but has been the sequel to struggles and blows.

In a small attic room, under a sky-light window, surrounded by all the circumstances that indicated indigence, isolation, and struggle, there was heard the click of the hammer upon a fine chisel, as it took from the marble block such delicate fragments that they fell as dust before the worker. The eye and face of the sculptor were almost those of an insane man. The suspended breath was followed by sighs of relief, only as now and then some partial success seemed to bring a single feature into harmony with the ideal of the brain.

Hours passed, and the man worked on. In the next garret a cobbler pegged away at his honest work, wondering how a man could thus be bothered, day by day, and week upon week, *simply to cut a stone to shape.* The sculptor died, and few followed him to his humble resting-place. His statue, the achievement of a life of struggle, lived on, and gave to his memory the savor of an honored name, and it became the model for copyists and worshipping admirers so long as time shall render tribute to art. Such is the memory of a faithful life, and in that devotion to work is epitomized the law for your struggle and mine. As the river, that bears great ships, and is tributary to the commerce of the world, is the aggregate of unnumbered minor streams, so its history is peculiar. It was not always the perfect, majestic moving agent of commerce. Some of its feeding tributaries gained birth in little springs, whose fountains had barely life enough to overflow their basins, or trickle from the mountain side, to strengthen, drop by drop, the nearest little brook. Sands absorbed and suns dried out much of their first expenditure of moisture. Summer showers, or the early meltings of the winter snow, rendered timely contributions, so that at last, all combined with other streams, alike of humble birth, to make that river. Work, progress, and the combination of all small agencies toward a common end, secured the result.

Thus began the struggle to achieve freedom for your race, and that noble man, Chief Justice

CHASE, who adorns the seat of Chief Justice
MARSHALL, attained his place by earnest work,
and, above all, that earnest work that endures
forever—consistent, constant work for Liberty
and Right.

Our individual life, from its beginning, has
been a struggle. We came into the world cry-
ing, wailing infants, as if conscious of life's trials
yet to come. The first struggle for a pair of
boots, for marbles, tops, or other boy-time toys
or amusements, was representative of the fact
that all acquirement was to be gained through
desire, labor, and struggle.

The ambition and competition, the quarrels
and jealousies of boyhood, youth, and manhood,
whether in study, amusement, or *work*, have all
had their natural place in this sphere of struggle.
There have been historic periods, characters, and
emergencies, when the distinctness, boldness, and
results of struggle have given names to dynasties,
characters, or issues, which for a time have re-
tained their prestige as memorable examples for
the information, warning, or encouragement of
other generations.

But, as a general law, as with the river, so it
is with States and races. The general result is
regarded by the world without regard to the individual elements that secured the result, until
Time's Avenger, the Judge of all the earth, shall
declare, before the assembled universe, the exact

measure of honor due even to the humblest of all
His creatures. Individuals are smothered in the
rubbish of the past, but the Omniscient Father
has in keeping the record of every thought or
deed that has advanced His glory.

If the islands of the Pacific, delivered from
the bowels of the earth by mighty upheavals of
the volcano or earthquake, have been fertilized
and planted through the visits of the birds of the
air, and from seeds borne across the ocean by the
winds of heaven, how much more certainly are
the small matters of daily duty to be traced forward and shaped by well-timed estimate of their
value, so that they may intelligently work to
the perfection of character and the blessing of
life.

One thought more just here.

The great victories of the battle-field have
almost always turned upon something so slight
that any other contingency would have lost the
issue. *How did the spade and pick-axe of plain,
honest farmers, ninety-three years ago, this very day,
give to Bunker Hill its glory?* How uncertain were
the waiting hours that, with Blucher's arrival,
gave to England her Waterloo! How, above
all strange, was that madness of passion which
evoked the American rebellion, and out of its
suppression perfected American liberty, and
gave to the world, at last, the example of one
free republic. That vast expenditure of blood

and treasure was made up of individual struggle, most of it unheralded and unhonored *by man ;* but in and through that struggle, there sprang forth in fresh beauty and glory, the secret of success for all individual or national endeavor, " *Devotion to Duty.*"

To your young men, I say that you are all sculptors, chipping out your fortunes. No man of any spirit, whether black or white, and having any just idea of his capacity and destiny, will be passively cast by others from any mould, nor will he accept, as satisfactory to himself, any result for his life that lacks the endurance of the real marble.

You are all, likewise, contributing your share to the momentum and volume of that great current of life which represents the republic, and which, flowing out over both oceans, bathes the shores and receives the out-flowing streams from other lands and people. You fight the battle of life and share a part in the great warfare that must culminate in victory for every faithful heart, and will realize its complete glory in an enfranchised world.

Take my well-intended counsels to your homes and to your daily work. You will get some impressions from what I say. You will have new responsibilities because of this interview. You cannot walk a rod and breathe the air you live in without receiving some impression upon your health and physical being. Not a drink of water passes your lips that has not its humble place in the economy of your active life. Yet a thankless soul regards neither with any proper regard for the Author of daily mercies, just as those who live on that belt of our earth beneath which the molten lava sways and surges, rebuild their frail habitations just so soon as the foundations cease to tremble from the earthquake, or the lava from the volcano has cooled sufficiently for their work.

You may go away to-night and forget, for the present, all I have said. Some who have not fully understood all will neglect to ask of others who did. The time will come when you will remember every wasted opportunity and every slighted counsel. It will be *your* fault, one and all, if you do not go away with *some* thought, *some new purpose, some fresh resolve* to be better and more useful planted deep down in your breast. You are responsible for the improvement of good advice just as much as for the proper use of hands that are given you for labor, and for obedience to that conscience which is established in your hearts to declare the right and reject the wrong. Many of you, I know, will treat this hour as a social occasion, quite pleasant as it passes, forgetful that every hour has its lesson and its duties, and that there is no escape from responsibility for the improvement of every occasion in which to gain fresh incentive to become stronger, purer, and better.

Remember that you are bound to take part in daily struggle whether you do or do not wish to do so. The winds of heaven are ever in motion. When you think all is silence, far above you there are ceaseless currents that affect your being, and nothing in the Universe of God is at rest.

When men do not praise Him, the bursting seed, the lifting grain, the speeding waters, the forming crystals, the absorbing leaves which live on dew and air, and those past generations of shells and vegetation, which have been so long maturing into limestone or coal for the use of man, are all lively at work, and unceasingly join in glad tribute to the Great Creator for His wisdom, goodness, power, and love.

Thus you must work and struggle, if you would attain any good thing. To be sure, it will not always be easy thus to work. There is no struggle and nothing gained when there is no opposition or resistance. Hence reward is held out to entice labor forward. There is no pursuit of an object in hand. There is no climbing of a mountain after the summit is reached. But *you* have not reached the end of life's pursuit, and every hour wasted is loss irreparable. Therefore, work on. Every passion, purpose, or desire of man only works toward its object through struggle. It is for each one of you, for me, and for every human soul to determine on what to expend effort; and to each soul is left the more solemn responsibility to see to it that he does not spend his strength for bubbles that burst in the grasp.

I have sufficiently occupied your time. *By forthcoming provisions of the Constitution of the Republic you will come into new spheres of activity and duty, and corresponding responsibilities will devolve upon you.*

In meeting you on this occasion, I cheerfully say that I hail with gladness the coming day of your matured freedom. I have felt it to be my duty, however feebly, to attempt to touch, here and there, some chord that would so vibrate as to leave a happy cadence sounding in your souls. Have you ever thought a moment how far little things travel, or how vast the range of mischief which single acts embrace? The disobedience of our first parents, the murder of ABEL, THE DISGRACE OF HAM, have each and all swept down the stream of time regardless of the flight of ages and the death of generations, and still these memorial sins rest heavy upon all who are now called upon to profit by the lessons those crimes inculcate. Let your acts and lives come so nearly to the requirements of duty that, through the blood of the Great Redeemer, you shall do your life's work acceptably, and be spared the curse that awaits the unprofitable servant.

It will soon be no novelty to have white men appointing places at which to meet and address you. I am here, casually, on duty as a soldier, and, I hope, a soldier of the Cross, as well as of my country. To refuse to address you upon the presumption that the soldier has no interest in your welfare which he could express, would have been to stultify my conscience, and refuse utterance to the hopes and expectations of thirty years, which are no longer matters of faith, but of speedy experience, as Freedom achieves its crowning triumphs in equal franchise for all. I have, therefore, in the spirit, as I believe, of the great religious interest which now pervades this people, told you plainly what seems to me to be a noble path for your steps to trace.

Though in a very few days I shall complete the duty which called me here, and I shall certainly never meet you all again, it is my earnest hope that He, whose temple you build, may meet you as you first assemble within its walls. Build it with open hands and willing hearts. Giving to God will enrich and not impoverish. When completed, let it be consecrated with the best gifts you can render, the gift of hearts.

So shall your life, when ended, go not out like some fading taper; but, catching radiance from the Heavens opened to receive you, the spirit shall quickly pass the skies, to shine afresh and forever in the transcendent effulgence of the Sun